KB086207

혜자의 눈꽃

도서출판 아시아에서는 《바이링궐 에디션 한국 대표 소설》을 기획하여 한국의 우수한 문학을 주제별로 엄선해 국내외 독자들에게 소개합니다. 이 기획은 국내외 우수한 번역가들이 참여하여 원작의 품격을 최대한 살렸습니다. 문학을 통해 아시아의 정체성과 가치를 살피는 데 주력해 온 도서출판 아시아는 한국인의 삶을 넓고 깊게 이해하는 데 이 기획이 기여하기를 기대합니다.

Asia Publishers presents some of the very best modern Korean literature to readers worldwide through its new Korean literature series 〈Bilingual Edition Modern Korean Literature〉. We are proud and happy to offer it in the most authoritative translation by renowned translators of Korean literature. We hope that this series helps to build solid bridges between citizens of the world and Koreans through a rich in-depth understanding of Korea.

바이링궐 에디션 한국 대표 소설 051

Bi-lingual Edition Modern Korean Literature 051

Hye-ja's Snow-Flowers

천승세
혜자의 눈꽃

Chun Seung-sei

ASIA
PUBLISHERS

Contents

혜자의 눈꽃

Hye-ja's Snow-Flowers

탐스러운 눈송이들이 하늘을 메우고 있었다.

어지러운 눈발 속에서 여인의 글썽한 눈이 보였다. 여인의 해들거리는 웃음을 봄 삼아 폈을, 어쩌면 그보다 먼저 힘겨운 목숨의 곁가시 위에 안쓰럽게 펴났을, 그 노랑색 꽃술의 눈꽃들은 이제 더는 피어나지 못할 것이었다.

눈물처럼 아리고 매운 궁금증이 하나 있었다.

혜자 할머니는 무슨 뜻으로 여인의 발걸음 뒤에다 꽃잎을 새겨주면서까지 여인의 힘겨운 나들이를 용서해 버렸는지 모른다.

The shroud of descending snow filled the entire sky.

I could see the woman's teary eyes amidst the descending streaks of snow. The snow-flowers and their yellow pistils would no longer bloom, the flowers that had bloomed as if it were spring amidst the backdrop of the woman's uncontrollable, vacant laughter, the flowers that had bloomed so pitifully on the struggling limb of that woman's fading life.

I was sorely curious about something, as sorely and intensely as that woman had cried.

I wondered why Hye-ja's grandmother had for-

그해 겨울의 인동(忍冬)은 음울함을 넘어 사뭇 슬프기까지 했었다.

그때 나는 삼동의 추위 속에서 이사를 해야 했을 정도로 삶의 옥죄이는 허기에 탈진되며 눅눅한 가난을 체험해봤던 것이다. 보증금 없이 월 이천 원 사글세의 셋방이라는 명목대로, 그해 그 눈 많던 겨울의 내 거처가 돼주었던 다행스러운 판잣집은, 우이동의 산자락을 비집는 황량한 공터에 달랑 앉아 있었다.

산언덕 위로는 요란스러운 고급 호텔이 늘편하게 앉아 있었고 산길을 겸한 좁은 길목이 똬리를 튼 처량한 한길이 나의 판잣집을 싸안으면서 산속으로 올라 뻗고 있었다.

담도 없이 한길과 맞 트인 마당(마당이라기보다는 사람의 손질이 미칠 새 없는 버려진 땅이라 해야 마땅할 것이다) 안으로는 보기 힘든 경색의 노송들이 울울하게 들어서 있었고 그 노송의 숲과 호텔이 앉아 있는 산언덕 발치께로 도봉동 한천으로 흐르고 있을 법한 시린 개울이 가만가만 달리고 있었던 거였다. 말하자면, 내 사글셋방의 마당 구실을 하고 있는 그 노송밭은 그 어느 땐가는 청청한 심곡 속이었을 것이나 개울이 파이면서 덩달아 한

given that woman for all her trouble and why she had had flower petals imprinted behind her footprints.

Honeysuckles that winter were not just depressing, but miserable and abject. I was so poor that winter that I had to move in the middle of one of the coldest winter months. I was poor in the kind of way that left me totally exhausted because it left me oppressively hungry. The shack that had fortunately offered me shelter that winter, a room that perfectly suited its shack description, "a rented room with no deposit required and a two thousand *won* monthly rent," sat alone in a desultory glade at the cramped foot of a mountain slope in Ui-dong. A gaudy-looking luxury hotel was perched leisurely atop that mountain. There was a pitiful thoroughfare that stretched upwards towards the mountaintop, curled around my shack and then curved at a narrow coiling corner of the mountain.

In the yard in front of my shack that opened towards the thoroughfare, there was a thick forest of old, rare pine trees. The yard really didn't deserve the name "yard;" it was a patch of land that hadn't been taken care of by human hands. At the foot of

길 쪽으로 밀려난 허진 풍치로 가늠해야 옳을 것이었다.

훈기 하나 없는 방에서 인동의 삭연한 잠을 보채이다가 선뜩해서 깨어나면, 노송들은 가지가 휘는 겨운 설화들을 얹고 있었고, 그 설화들의 밀밀한 틈새에서 다시 태어나는 눈부신 햇살들이 스멀대는 솔잎 그늘을 올올이 적시며 눈밭에 와 닿아 있곤 했다.

나는 이 노송밭의 설화들과 시리디 시린 아침 햇살에 취해 가슴 저리는 가난도 잊고 있었다. 이런 경치에다가 굳이 하나를 더 보탠다면, 나의 판잣집 뒷 봉창께로 바짝 잇대어 뻗는 산길도 무척 좋았다.

눈밭을 밟는 발작 소리들이 사각사각 봉창을 흔들 때면 나는 화급스레 일어나 봉창 문턱에다 턱을 얹곤 했었는데, 형형색색의 차림들로 산속을 향해 걷는 등산객들의 모습은 어찌 보면 조금씩 허물어져 내리는 눈사태 위를 밀리는 꽃덤불을 보는 듯한 착각마저 일으켜주곤 하던 것이다.

그들의 무리들이 모두 산속으로 빨려들고 산길이 휑 빌 때쯤이면 나는 노송밭을 걸어 찢긴 얼음결 속에서 졸졸졸 소리를 내며 흐르는 그 개울까지 걸어가 사위를 맴돌이하며 서 있다 돌아오곤 했다.

this forest and the hotel-topped mountain, a cold brook flowed serenely downstream, perhaps, towards the Han Creek in Dobong-dong. In other words, that old pine tree forest that played the role of my shack's yard must have once been a fresh, green remote mountain area, and it had had now become a part of an uncertain landscape after having been pushed towards the thoroughfare when the brook first formed.

When I would awake in that freezing room after a fitful night, I used to find old pine trees bearing snow-flowers on their branches, the branches straining under the weight of the snow and their fruit. The sunshine would bear in between the crowded snow-flowers, wet the rustling pine needle shades, and touch the snowfield.

Drunk with those snow-flowers and the old pine tree field and those freezing morning sunrays, I was sometimes able to forget the stinging state of my poverty. Also, if I might add one more element to this landscape, I loved the mountain trail that stretched right under the sealed window of my room.

Whenever I'd hear footsteps crunch through the snowfield and rattle my window, I would spring out

산언덕 위의 고급 호텔도 마냥 적적함만을 다스리고 앉아 있는 품이 계절 탓인 듯싶었고, 인가라야 개울 끝 산기슭에 앉은 판잣집이 또 하나 있을 뿐이어서, 하늘을 우러러 맴돌이를 하는 귓가로는 졸졸졸 흐르는 개울 소리와 그 개울 소리에 섞이는 간간한 잣새 울음들이 고작이었다. 그래서 노송밭 아래로 수북이 쌓인 눈길(한길과 개울 끝까지의 넓이로 트인 눈밭이라야 옳다) 위로는 언제나 나의 발자국이 천진한 산짐승의 조심스러운 나들이처럼 그렇게 첫 번째 발도장을 찍었으며 나는 이 첫 번째의 내 발자국이 좋아 눈을 뜨기가 무섭게 노송밭을 걸어왔던 것이었다.

그날도 나는 개울가의 왕돌 위에 앉아 사위를 두리번거리며 콧속이 바직거릴 정도로 신뜩한 새벽 공기를 마시고 있었다.

사위를 두리번거리는 내 눈 안으로 드는 것은 내 사글셋방 쪽에서부터 개울까지 나란히 파인 긴 내 발자국들과 잣새들의 푸득거림에 흩날리는 눈가루, 그리고 그 잣새들을 날려 보내고 난 영근 솔잎들의 하들하들 떨어대는 연한 미동들이었다.

나는 개울가 쪽으로 바짝 잇대어 길게 새겨진 또 하

of my bed and lay my chin on the windowsill. The hikers in their colorful outfits made me feel as if I was looking at flowering shrubs sliding down on top of a slowly crumbling avalanche. Around the time when all the hikers were lost in the depths of the mountain and the trail emptied out, I began to walk across the old pine forest to the bank of the brook that trickled down under the torn layers of ice, survey the environment for a while, and then return to my room.

Perhaps because it was the off-season, the luxury hotel was resting leisurely and trying to enjoy its solitude. There was only one other shack at the end of the brook at the foot of the mountain. All I could hear was the sound of the brook trickling down the mountain slopes and the crying of the crossbills. Occasionally, the sound of the crossbills mixed with the sound of the brook. So, when I would venture from my home I would always leave the first footprints on the snow-piled path under the old pine field, my footprints like those of an innocent mountain animal on its first outing. I loved making those first footprints so much that I would rush out to walk on that old pine field as soon as I'd open my eyes.

나의 발자국들을 보다 말고 피식 웃었다. 그 앙증맞을 정도로 작은 발자국들은 개울 끝 쪽의 판잣집을 향해 촘촘히 뻗고 있다.

'혜자라는 그 애 발자국이군.'

나는 그 작은 발자국들의 모양을 유심히 내려다보면서 그 애가 눈밭 위를 깡충깡충 뛰어갔을 것이라는 싱거운 짐작을 곁들이고 있었다. 그 작고 예쁜 발자국들은 왕돌더미 바로 앞에서 시작되고 있었는데 얼마간 또 륵또륵 이어지다가 이내 폭을 넓히며 들쑥날쑥 멀어지고 있기 때문이었다. 몇 번 먼 눈어림 속에다 담아봤던 그 혜자라는 계집아이의 모습이 떠오르는 듯도 싶었다. 그 애는 바지 주머니에다 두 손을 찌른 채 깡충깡충 뛰어 제 집으로 돌아가곤 했다. 그럴 때면 그 애의 짧은 무릎께에까지 뿌연 눈가루가 일고 털모자 끝에서 달랑대는 털실 방울이 시계추처럼 좌우로 나풀거리던 것이다.

내가 이런 생각을 하며 왕돌 위에서 내려섰을 때였을 것이었다. 별안간 차디찬 여인의 웃음소리가 까들까들 울려왔다. 내가 소리 나는 쪽을 향해 등 돌아섰을 때 그 웃음소리는 뚜욱 멎었다. 내가 노송밭 쪽으로 몇 발짝 걸음을 옮겨놨을 때 그 웃음소리는 다시 간드러졌다.

One particular day, while I sat atop a large rock near the brook and surveyed my surroundings, I was just taking in the early morning air—so cold it made my nostrils freeze and crack. But then I noticed a long train of my parallel footprints that stretched from the shack of my rented room to the brook. The powdery snow swirled upwards with the fluttering of crossbills and the gentle shaking of the ripe pine needles that sent them on their way.

I smiled when I saw another long train of small footprints right next to the brook. Those tiny footprints continued in a dense line towards the other shack at the end of the brook. "Those must be that child Hye-ja's footprints." As I stared at the tracks and thought this, I also wondered about the manner in which the child must have hopped through the snowfield. Those diminutive footprints began right in front of the large rock, continued at a regular interval for a while, and then zigzagged off in larger leaps. I could almost picture that young girl whom I had seen from afar a few times. When I'd usually see her, she'd be in the middle of hopping back towards her house, her two hands in her pant pockets. Every time I'd see her go, the snow would rise up to her tiny knees and the dangling pom-

나는 다시 돌아섰다. 그 웃음소리는 너무나 기척이 없어 언제나 빈집만 같던 개울 끝 쪽의 그 판잣집 속에서 울려나오고 있는 듯싶었다. 그 웃음소리는 내가 돌아서면 멎고 집으로 걸음을 옮길 때면 다시 울리곤 했는데 번번이 그 웃음을 만들어내고 있는 사람의 형체는 찾아볼 수가 없었다.

나는 걷는 체하다가 그 웃음소리가 막 울리기 시작했을 때 별안간 휑 돌아섰다. 여인의 상반신이 그 판잣집의 낮은 블록담 안으로 막 감춰지고 있었다. 나는 몽롱한 정신으로 잠시 그렇게 서 있었다. 담 위로 여인의 머리가 스른스런 떠오르고 있었다. 여인은 내 쪽을 바라다보며 또 한 차례 간드러지는 웃음을 터뜨려놓고 나서 다시 머리통을 담 안으로 삼췄다. 여인의 머리가 다시 담 위에 얹혔을 때 혜자의 할머니일 성싶은 사람이 방문을 차고 우르르 마당으로 내려서는 듯싶었다. 그녀의 주먹이 여인의 머리통을 한두 번 쥐어박고 있었다.

"이구 웬수, 웬수우─."

낮은 투정이 건너왔다.

나는 여인의 웃음과 풀 죽은 투정이 그친 그 판잣집을 곁눈질로 흘려보내며 집을 향해 걸음을 옮겼다.

poms on top of her knit hat would swing back and forth like the pendulum on a clock.

When I stepped down from the large rock, I suddenly heard a woman's coquettish, yet icy cold laughter. When I turned in the direction of laughter, it suddenly stopped. When I resumed my walk and took a few steps towards the old pine field, there was that laughter again. Once more, I turned around. The laughter seemed to be coming from the shack at the end of the brook, the one that was so quiet that it seemed like it was always empty. The sound stopped whenever I turned around and then resumed whenever I continued on a few steps. But every time I turned I could never see anyone making that laughter.

Finally, I pretended to walk and then whirled around when the laughter began again. I was just able to catch a glimpse of the upper half of a woman's body hiding below the low concrete block wall in front of one of the shacks. Bewildered, I stood still for a while until a woman's head slowly emerged from behind the wall. She looked in my direction and then laughed shyly and flirtatiously before hiding her head back under the wall. When her head was out from behind the wall again,

그러던 어느 날이었다.

나는 노송밭께로 트인 창문 밖에서 이는 도란대는 기척을 듣고 자리에서 일어났다. 눈이 부신 햇살이 유리창에 낀 성에를 녹이는 품이 어느 때보다도 아침이 익어버린 듯싶었다.

아침이 그새 익어버렸다면 노송밭 아래의 눈밭 위로는 주인집 할머니의 발자국이 벌써 첫 번째의 발도장을 찍어댔을 것이려니 하는 생각에 미쳐 나는 맥이 풀리는 기분이었다.

나는 일어서려다 말고 잠시 앉은 채로 뭉그적거렸다. 참으로 야릇한 조형이 성에 낀 유리창을 수놓고 있었기 때문이었다.

가늘고 긴 손가락이었다. 그 손가락은 성에가 낀 유리창을 화판 삼아 그림을 그려대고 있는 듯도 싶었고 서툰 글씨를 써대고 있는 듯도 싶었다.

사각사각 쓰르르 사각—

나는 그 손가락의 동작 끝에 열리는 이런 소리를 들으며 허망한 도리질을 해봤다.

'누구람. 여태 한 번도 이런 적이 없었는데. 아, 개울 끝 판잣집에 사는 그 혜자라는 어린애인 모양이군,

a woman that looked like Hye-ja's grandmother kicked the door of a room open and rushed out to the yard. She rapped the head of the woman a couple of times.

"Oh, dear, you, my nemesis, you!" She made a low grumbling sound. I threw a sidelong glance at that shack and then walked back towards my shack.

A few days passed.

I woke up when I heard a whispering sound outside the window facing the old pine field. From the look of the bright sunrays melting the frost on the window, it appeared to be mid-morning.

Since it was mid-morning, I knew that there would already be the grandmother's footprints under the old pine trees on the snowfield. I felt dejected.

I did not feel like standing up, so I lounged around on the floor instead. But then, an odd shape silhouetted my bedroom window.

I saw a very thin, long finger. It seemed to be drawing something on the frost of my window. Or, maybe it was writing something.

"Sagaksagak Ssururu Sagak..." I listened to these sounds that accompanied the movements of the

……아니지. 그 계집아이는 노송밭을 걸어 이쪽으로 와본 적이 한 번도 없었는데…… 그리고 유리창에다 무늬를 새길 만큼 키가 크질 않는데……'

나는 이런 생각을 하다 말고 부스스 일어나 유리창께로 다가갔다. 그리고 드르륵 창문을 열었다.

창문 아래에는 웬 여인이 서 있었다. 그 여인 옆에 한두 번 본 적이 있는 혜자라는 계집아이가 바짝 붙어 서 있었다.

여인은 검지 끝을 입술로 문 채 나를 빤히 올려다보고 있었고 혜자라는 계집아이는 내 얼굴에 못 박고 있던 눈길을 거둬 제 발치께를 내려다보고 있었다.

나는 그녀의 검지 끝이 입술에 물려 있는 점으로 미루어 성에가 낀 유리창을 화판 삼아 무늬를 그리고 있었던 사람이 이 여인이라고 단정 짓고 있었다. 창문이 열리는 통에 화급스레 거뒀던 시린 손가락 끝을 입김으로 녹이고 있는 것이라고ㅡ.

"……누구신지요?"

"……."

여인은 해들해들 웃으며 나를 똑바로 올려다보고 있을 뿐이었다. 여인의 창백한 이마 위로 잔잔하게 흔들

finger and shook my head. Who could it be? Nothing like this had ever happened before. Maybe it was that girl Hye-ja from the shack at the end of the brook. No. She never walked across the old pine field in this direction. Besides, she wasn't tall enough to reach this window to draw something on it.

I got up slowly, and walked towards the window. Without much warning, I threw it open.

A woman was standing below it. Beside her stood the girl, Hye-ja, whom I had seen a couple of times by then, standing right behind her.

The woman was staring up at me, biting the tip of her forefinger, and the girl, Hye-ja, who had been staring at me, was looking down at her own feet.

Because the woman was biting the tip of her forefinger, I decided that she was the one who had been drawing something on my window. She must have been warming the freezing tip of her finger with her breath, the finger she must have had pulled back abruptly because I had just opened the window.

"Who are you?" The woman didn't answer but simply stared up at me, smiling coquettishly. The

23

리는 솔잎들이 그늘지고 있었다.

"하긴 그렇군요. ……저를 찾아오셨을 리가 없겠군요. 우리는 서로 모르는 사이일 테니깐 말입니다. 아, 그렇군요. 모르는 사이라기보다는 몰라야 옳겠습니다."

나는 바보스럽게 중얼대며 뒤통수를 긁적거렸다. 여인은 예의 해들거리는 웃음을 흘리고 선 채 신기한 구경이라도 하는 듯 나의 얼굴 구석구석을 면밀히 뜯어보고 있었다.

백지장처럼 새하얀 얼굴. 크고 맑되 생기가 없는 눈. 그리고 퍼런 힘줄이 드러나도록 깡마른 손목―나는 치마 끝에 드러난 여인의 맨발을 내려다보며 섬뜩한 추위를 느끼고 있었다.

여인의 눈이 금세 글썽기리고 있었다. 여인의 긴 속눈썹이 축축한 눈물에 젖어들며 파들파들 떨리기 시작했을 때 혜자는 묻지도 않은 말을 했다. 혜자는 발로 앙증맞은 눈꽃을 새겨가면서 천천히 맴돌이를 시작했다.

"우리 엄마예요."

"……"

"많이 많이 아파요."

"……"

pine needles were trembling gently, drawing thin shadows over her pale forehead.

"Oh, that's right. You're not here to see me. We don't know each other. That's right. It's not that we don't know each other, but that we shouldn't know each other," I scratched the back of my head. The woman was still smiling at me in the same way and studying my facial features very carefully now, as if she was looking at something very interesting. Her face was almost as white as a sheet of paper. Her eyes were large and clear, but inanimate. And her skinny wrists displayed blue veins. Just looking at the woman's bare feet, I felt terribly cold.

Her eyes suddenly filled with tears. Just when her long eyelashes began to grow wet and tremble, Hye-ja piped up. She slowly spun around and drew snow-flowers with her round, tiny feet in the snow.

"This is my mom," she said.

I didn't know what to say.

"She is very very ill."

I still didn't know how to respond.

"Please let us go. Quick! If Grandma finds out about this, we're in big trouble."

Still not knowing what to say, I just stood there

"빨리 가게 해주세요. ……할머니가 보면 큰일 나요."

나는 무슨 말을 해야 할지 몰라 눈길만 두리번거리며 바보처럼 서 있을 뿐이었다. 여인은 그 글썽한 눈을 들고 마침 노송의 가지 사이를 날며 깍깍대는 한 쌍의 까치를 올려다봤다.

내가 어떻든 무슨 말이든지 해야 할 것이라고. 그래서 이 꿈속만 같은 정황을 우선 벗어나야 할 것이라고 생각하며 막 여인을 똑바로 내려다봤을 때, 혜자 할머니가 바쁜 걸음으로 노송밭을 질러오고 있었다. 혜자 할머니는 하늘 속을 우러러 몇 번 긴 한숨을 내뿜고 나서 깊은 팔짱을 꼈다. 그녀의 침울한 눈길이 여인과 혜자를 물끄러미 건너다보고 있었다.

"에미 니 뭘 하고 있니?"

"……"

"빨랑 안 돌아가겠니?"

혜자 할머니가 여인께로 성큼 다가들자 그제야 여인은 가녀린 등짝을 움츠리며 풀이 죽어 돌아섰다. 여인은 걸음을 옮기다 말고 잠시 돌아서선 나를 향해 손을 내흔들었다.

"저런 웬수년 허구는. 쯔읏 쯔읏— 그새 여긴 왜 왔담.

like a fool and looked around helplessly. The woman looked up, her eyes still tearful, and seemed to be looking up at a pair of magpies that were flying and cawing around the old pine trees. Finally, I looked straight down at the woman, thinking that I should say something and get out of this dream-like situation, when I saw Hye-ja's grandmother crossing the old pine field in a cloud of hurried steps. When she arrived at my shack she looked up at the sky and sighed deeply a few times. She folded her arms. She looked at Hye-ja and her mother, her eyes seemingly depressed.

"Dear, what are you doing here?" she finally asked.

No answer.

"Why don't you go back home quick?"

Only when Hye-ja's grandmother quickly approach the woman, did she shrink back and turn around, disheartened. As she walked back, she stopped for a moment, turned around towards me, and waved her hand.

"My nemesis! Tsk tsk! Why on earth did you come here? Do you think you're still a woman, huh? Looking at a man and feeling horny, huh?" Hye-ja's mother was staggering back, looking back

꼴에 계집값 허겠다구 원. ……낯선 사내를 보니깐 목
숨이 그저 동허나보지!"

여인은 흘끔흘끔 뒤를 살피며 비틀비틀 걷고 있었고
여인의 뒤를 바짝 잇대어 혜자 할머니가 잰걸음을 놓고
있었다. 여인은 포수의 총에 맞은 사슴이 잔명의 가쁜
숨을 헉헉대며 비틀대듯 그렇게 눈밭을 질러가고 있었
다.

나는 멀어져가는 그들을 한동안 망연히 내려다보고
있었다. 내가 방문을 나섰을 때 주인집 할머니가 방문
을 열고 얼굴을 내밀었다.

"누가 왔었수?"

"글쎄요…… 처음 보는 여자인데요."

"혜자 어미가 왔었던 게로군…… 이구 쯔웃 쯔웃―
고게 어쩌자구 저리 목숨이 길어설랑 저 고생인구. 폐
병 말기에다 정신병마저 겹쳐설랑 오늘내일하는 앤
데…… 먼발치로 선상님을 봤던 게로군. 그래 안 오던
여길 다 왔지. 죽을려니깐 사람이 그리워져 저렇지."

나는 주인 할머니의 말을 등 뒤로 흘리며 개울을 향
해 걷기 시작했다. 까치가 낮게 날 때마다 설화들은 뿌
연 눈가루가 되어 흩어져 내렸다.

frequently while Hye-ja's grandmother followed close behind her with small, quick steps. The woman was crossing the snowy field like a reeling deer, short of breath as if she had just been shot by a hunter's gun.

I stared at them blankly as they walked away. As I was about to go outside, my landlady opened her door and poked her head out.

"Did someone just drop by?" she asked.

"Well, it was a woman I haven't seen before."

"That must be Hye-ja's mom. Oh, tsk tsk. How come she has to cling to life so that she has to suffer so much? She's got tuberculosis and so she's at death's door but, besides that, she's also just crazy. She must have seen you from far away. That must be why she came here. She's never headed this way before. She must miss people now that she's about to die."

Before she finished her sentence, I began to walk towards the brook. Whenever magpies flew low, the snow-flowers became snow powder and sprinkled all over the field.

I walked, looking down at the haphazard footprints that stretched across the old pine field to my room for the first time since I had moved in. Then,

나는 이사 온 후 처음으로 노송밭을 질러 내 방 앞까지 줄을 이은 어지러운 발자국을 내려다보며 걸었다. 그러다가 주춤 굳어 섰다. 개울 쪽에서부터 이쪽까지 다섯 개의 눈꽃들이 그 어지러운 발자국들 틈에 새겨져 있는 것이었다. 그 눈꽃들은 앙증맞도록 작은 발자국이 맴을 돌며 꽃잎의 결을 새겨가고 있었는데, 그 눈꽃의 한가운데쯤에는 노란색 물이 번져 있어, 마치 노란색 꽃술에서부터 꽃잎이 피고 있는 듯한 조밀스러운 것이었다.

　나는 왕돌 위에 올라 여느 때처럼 큰 숨을 들이마시면서 노송밭을 비끼는 바람결처럼 차디찬 웃음을 가들지게 떨었던 그 여인이 바로 혜자 엄마라고 다짐했다.

　오랜만에 호텔로 오르는 길목에 빨강색 승용차 한 대가 얹혀 있었다. 그 자동차는 하얀 선백의 꽃대공을 타오르는 딱정벌레처럼 사뭇 기어대고 있었다.

　그날 이후, 여인은 두 번을 더 내 방 유리창 앞까지 찾아와 성에 낀 유리창을 화판 삼아 야릇한 조형을 손가락으로 새겨놓고 갔다. 여인은 첫 번 때와 마찬가지로 나를 올려다보면 해들거렸고 또 금세 글썽이는 눈이 되

suddenly, I stopped. In between the footprints, there were five snow-flowers between the brook and my shack. The snow-flowers had been made with someone else's dainty whirling footprints. There were yellow spots in the middle of these flowers, which made them look as if dense petals were spread around the yellow pistils. I stepped up on a large rock and breathing in deeply. I concluded that the woman who'd been laughing in that coquettish and chilling manner, like the sound of the wind blowing through the old pine field, was none other than Hye-ja's mom.

A red sedan was making its way towards the hotel. It had been awhile since anyone had seen a car on that road. The car was crawling up the mountain like a ladybug climbing up a white flower stalk.

Since that day, the woman came to my room window two more times, drawing strange figures on the window's frosty surface with her finger each time before she left. Just like the first time, she looked up at me, smiling coquettishly, until her eyes filled with tears. The only change was that she now spoke to me. All she said was, "How are you?"

"How are You?"

곤 했으나, 한 가지 달라진 게 있다면 여인이 말을 하게 된 일이었다. 그 말이란 것이 밑도 끝도 없이 반복되는 "안녕하세요!" 하는 이 한마디였다.

"안녕하세요!"

"네에, 안녕하셨습니까."

"안녕하세요!"

"네에, 안녕했습니다."

"안녕하세요!"

"네에."

"안녕하세요!"

"……네에……."

"안녕하세요!"

"……."

나는 대답하기에 기진해서 끝내는 솔잎 새로 부챗살을 펴는 부신 햇살을 바라다보기 일쑤였으나 여인은 구관조처럼 부지런히도 "안녕하세요!"를 되뇌던 것이었다.

나는 여인의 "안녕하세요!"라는 말에 지치면 그럴수록 혜자의 거동에 흥미를 느끼곤 했다.

내가 창문을 드르륵 열고 얼굴을 내밀 때면 그때마다

"I'm fine, and you?"

"How are you?"

"I'm fine, and you?"

"How are you?"

"I'm fine."

"How are you?"

"...I'm fine."

"How are you?"

Eventually, I could no longer answer.

Although I got tired of answering the same question over and over again, and just looking at the bright sun rays spreading like a fan among the pine needles, she repeated "How are you?" as diligently as a myna.

The more tired I grew of the woman's "How are you?" the more interested I became in Hye-ja's behavior.

Whenever I opened my window wide and stuck my face out, Hye-ja was standing right behind the woman, looking bleak and pitiful, unbecoming of her age.

Sometimes, the woman shuffled back and forth on the narrow path, repeatedly muttering "How are you?" to herself. Hye-ja would follow close behind, always only looking down. Interestingly, Hye-ja

혜자는 꼭 여인의 엉덩이 뒤쪽에 바짝 붙어 있곤 했는데 그런 혜자의 모습은 나이에 걸맞지 않게 너무나 음울하고 측은해 뵈던 것이다.

여인은 "안녕하세요!"를 되뇌며 간혹 좁은 거리를 오락가락하기도 했다. 그럴 때면 혜자는 여인의 뒤를 바짝바짝 따르며 얼굴을 떨구고 있었는데 혜자의 눈길은 신통스럽게도 여인이 밟고 지나간 눈밭에만 못 박혀 있을 뿐 다른 데를 보진 않던 것이다.

나는 여인의 해들거리는 웃음과 그 웃음 뒤에 금세 글썽이는 크고 맑은 눈을 내려다보면서, 그리고 혜자의 그 근심이 그려지는 눈길을 정탐하면서, 새벽같이 새기던 눈밭 위의 내 발자국을 점점 잊어가고 있었다. 내 크고 넓은 발자국보다는 여인의 걸음을 따르며 새겨지는 그 앙증맞은 눈꽃들이 더 좋아졌다고나 할까.

혜자는 여인이 나를 올려다보고 있는 동안에 대개 눈발 흩뿌리는 하늘 속이나 아니면 솔잎 새를 깡충대는 잣새들을 올려다보며 가쁜 입김을 푸우푸우 뿜어대곤 했다.

그럴 때면 내가 물었다.

"눈꽃은 네가 새기는 거지?"

looked only at the snowy path her captivated mother followed.

As I watched the woman and followed after her with my eyes, spying on Hye-ja and her anxious eyes as well, I began to forget the footprints I used to make early every morning. I was probably becoming fonder of those tiny snow-flowers imprinted behind the woman's footprints than my own large, clumsy tracks.

While the woman looked up at me, Hye-ja mostly looked up at the snow-filled sky or the crossbills moving amongst the pine needles, puffing and gasping as they leapt from branch to branch.

Sometimes, I would ask little Hye-ja, "You're the one who made those snow-flowers, right?"

"I don't know," she'd reply.

"Why do you make them?"

"Just because..."

Those were always Hye-ja's answers.

Smiling foolishly, I tried to understand her reasons on my own, the reason why Hye-ja followed so closely behind her mother and made snow-flowers with her feet. And I was even more curious about the yellow pistils right in the middle of those snow-flowers. It was clear that she drew those

"……몰라요……."

"눈꽃은 왜 새기니?"

"……그냥요……."

혜자의 대답은 언제나 "몰라요" "그냥요"였다.

나는 바보스럽게 웃으며 내 나름대로 궁금증을 풀어 보려고 애썼다. 그 궁금증이란, 혜자는 왜 여인의 뒤만 바짝바짝 따르며 그 같은 눈꽃들을 새기는 것인가 하는 것이었다. 그리고 그보다 더 궁금한 것은 그 눈꽃들의 한가운데서 피고 있는 노란색 꽃술이던 거였다. 꽃잎이야 발로 새긴다고 치고 그 노란색 물감은 따로 가지고 다니며 눈꽃의 한가운데다가 색을 들이는 것인가, 그런 짓은 혜자가 스스로 하는 짓인가, 아니면 여인이 시켜서 하는 짓일까.

나는 이런 궁금증을 밝혀내보려고 무진 애를 쓰는 편이었으나 혜자의 손에는 물감이 들려 있어본 적이 없었고 그 눈꽃은 여인이 다녀간 뒤면 으레 대여섯 송이가 흐드러지게 피어나던 것이었다. 앙증맞도록 귀여운 작은 발자국 꽃잎을 달고―.

어느 날 밤이었다. 솔가지가 보채이도록 바람결이 드셌다. 설화의 무더기가 땅으로 내리는지 간간이 퍽, 퍼

petals with her feet, but did she carry yellow dye to color each flower's center? Was it Hye-ja herself who did that? Or was it her mom who made her do that?

I tried very hard to find out the answer to these questions, but I never saw any colors or dye in Hye-ja's hands. Yet, there were always five or six snow-flowers blooming after each of her visits. Each flower would always hold those tiny, adorable footprint petals.

One night, a fierce wind arose that shook the pine branches mercilessly. My window echoed the sound of the snow-flowers falling from trees. The trees deep in the mountain seemed to be snapping their own branches off, unable to support the weight of snow piling on top of them. I could hear the sound of branch's snapping mixed with the sound of wind.

I was trying very hard to fall asleep, fighting off the cold drafts seeping through the cracks of my window, when, suddenly, I heard a strange sound near the window.

"Sagak sagak ssururu sagak..."

Slowly, I pulled myself into an upright position in my bed. I lit a candle and held it up to see outside.

억대며 봉창이 울었다. 먼 산속의 수목들이 쌓이는 눈을 못 이겨 가지를 찢는 모양이었다. 생지 부러지는 소리도 어쩌다가 바람결에 섞여왔다.

나는 봉창 사이로 스며드는 한기를 다스리며 잠을 청하려고 무척 애를 쓰고 있었다. 그러는데 창문께에서 야릇한 기척이 있었다.

사각 사각 스르르 사각—

나는 부스스 일어나 앉았다. 성냥을 찾아 촛불을 밝히고 창문께를 비춰 봤다. 가늘고 긴 손가락이 성에를 긁어내며 예의 야릇한 무늬를 새기고 있었다.

여인의 밤중 방문은 아침과 달리 무척 섬뜩하게 느껴지는 것이었다. 순간, 나는 여인의 하얀 맨발을 떠올리며 나도 몰래 모진 한속을 탔다. 나는 창께로 다가가 촛불이 바람에 꺼지지 않도록 창문을 조금만 열고 그 새로 얼굴을 내밀었다. 창을 밝히는 희뿌연 촛불의 산광이 여인의 얼굴을 희미하게 밝혀주고 있었다.

"아안녀엉하세요오. 아안녀엉하세요오"

추위 탓이었을 것이었다. 여인은 소름끼치도록 빠르게 턱을 떨며 겨우 목소리를 잇고 있었다.

나는 한동안 멍청하게 서 있다가 말했다.

A long, thin finger was scratching the frosty surface of my room window and drawing the same figure it used to draw.

Receiving a visit from this woman at night chilled me, unlike when she visited me during the daytime. Picturing her naked pale feet in my mind, I felt goosebumps all over. I went to the window, opened the window just a little so that the candle wouldn't get blown out, and peered outside. A diffused, misty light barely outlined the woman's face from the candle I held over the window.

"Ho-o-w-a-re-yo-ou-u, ho-o-w-a-re-yo-ou-u..."

Most likely because of the cold, the woman was barely managing to finish her sentences. Her teeth were chattering so hard they sent more chills down my spine.

I stood, staring blankly at her for a while, and finally replied, "You shouldn't be doing this... It's very cold outside... Why don't you come tomorrow morning and draw a picture...?"

"Ho-o-w-a-re-yo-ou-u..." she called again.

"If you keep standing out there like that on that snowfield, you'll be in big trouble. No, that's not even it. A person might freeze to death standing

"이러시면 안 되지요. ……날이 굉장히 춥군요. ……
내일 아침에 오셔서 그림을 그려주시지요……."

"……안녀엉하세요오―."

"그 눈밭에 그냥 서 계시다가는 큰일이 납니다. 아니
큰일 정도가 아닐는지도 모르지요. 사람이 얼어 죽을는
지도 모르지 않겠습니까!"

"안녀엉하세요오―."

"돌아가셔야 합니다. 어서요, 어서 돌아가세요."

여인은 전신을 부들부들 떨어대며 "안녕하세요!"만
열심히 되뇌고 있었다. 바람결에 흩날리는 여인의 머리
칼이 여름 오르내리는 파랫발처럼 이마를 덮다가 볼에
감기우다가 했다. 안타까움을 졸이며 어찌 할 바를 몰
라 섰던 나는 그제야 흠칫 놀랐다. 여인의 곁에 혜자가
없던 것이었다.

'아, 자고 있겠군. 혜자는 자고 있을 거야.'

나는 이런 생각을 하다 말고 다소 짜증스러워졌다. 여
인은 쉽게 물러갈 기미가 아니었다. 그렇다고 살을 에
는 바람결 속에다가 여인을 세워두고 모른 체 잠들 수
는 없는 일이었다.

나는 여인을 집에까지 바래다줘야 한다고 다짐하며

outside like that, don't you think so?"

"Ho-o-w-a-re-yo-ou-u…"

"You have to go back," I tried to speak firmly. "Quick! Now!"

The woman was trembling even harder now and continued repeating herself. Her hair danced in the wind and eventually covered her forehead, then covered her cheeks like kelp bobbing up and down amongst a rock beneath the waves. I stood there nervously now, helpless. Surprised, I suddenly realized something at that moment: Hye-ja was nowhere to be seen.

She must be sleeping, I thought. Hye-ja must be sleeping now. I began to get a little annoyed. The woman didn't look like she would be going away any time soon. Still, I couldn't just go back to sleep and let her keep standing there in the middle of that piercing wind. I had to take her back to her shack. I got ready to leave my room. When I got outside and approached her, she quickly drew back a few steps.

"No, I'm not going! I won't!"

I was surprised that her voice was unexpectedly loud and stubborn.

"That's too bad. You have to go home. Are you

방을 나왔다. 내가 여인의 곁에 다가섰을 때 여인은 서
너 발짝 화급스럽게 물러섰다.

"안 가! 안 가!"

"……?"

나는 여인의 목소리가 생각 밖으로 크고 완강한 것에
대해 놀라고 있었다.

"참 딱한 일입니다. 집으로 돌아가야지요. 그럼 이 눈
밭에 서서 밤을 새우겠다는 얘깁니까? ……어서 돌아
가세요. 어서요."

나는 멋쩍게 돌아서며 선백의 눈밭 위에 둥치를 박고
선 우람한 노송들을 내다봤다.

그때 멀지 않은 노송의 둥치 뒤에서 웬 그림자가 어른
대는가 싶었다. 그 그림자는 이내 눈밭 위로 모습을 니
타냈다. 그림자가 후적후적 이쪽으로 걸어오고 있었다.

그림자는 혜자 할머니였다.

혜자 할머니는 내 앞을 말없이 지나쳐 여인께로 다가
갔다. 그녀의 손이 여인의 등짝을 사납게 떠다밀고 있었
다. 여인이 비틀대며 내 앞을 지나쳐갔다. 혜자 할머니
는 저만큼 멀어지면서 그제야 낮게 투정하는 것이었다.

"웬수년, 웬수녀언— 내가 뭐래던. 네년이 사람인 줄

saying that you're going to stay up all night, standing in this snowfield? Come on, let's go back. Hur-
ry!" I turned around awkwardly and looked at the
magnificent old pine trees that stood strong over
the snowy field.

At that moment, I noticed a shadow seemingly
lingering behind an old pine not too far away. The
shadow soon revealed its shape in the field. It was
fast approaching. It was Hye-ja's grandmother.

She passed by me silently and walked up to the
woman. She began pushing the woman from behind roughly. The woman stumbled past me. When
they were a small distance away, Hye-ja's grandmother finally grumbled under her breath: "Oh, my
nemesis, you really are... What did I tell you? Do
you think you're a human being? ... That you're a
human being just because you're alive? Oh, dear...
What crime did I ever commit that I deserved this?"

I returned to my room and lay down, pulling the
comforter over my head. The gray shadow of Hye-
ja's grandmother behind the old pine trunk grew
and grew along with the incomprehensible words
she'd said outside.

My window grayed at dawn and filled with snow-

알았지? ……숨줄이 그적 붙어 있기 망정이지 네년이 사람인 줄 알았어? 이구우— 내가 무슨 죄로 이런 업을 당헌담!"

나는 방에 돌아와 이불을 머리끝까지 뒤집어쓰고 누워버렸다. 혜자 할머니가 내뱉던 뜻 모를 소리들에 어울리며 노송 둥치 뒤에 숨어 있던 그녀의 회색빛 그림자가 크게 크게 자라기만 하던 것이었다.

회색빛으로 트여오는 창 안에 눈발들만 가득히 메워지고 있었다. 나는 새벽이 익기 시작했을 때부터 유리창에다 질긴 눈길을 주고 있었으나 야릇한 조형의 시작은 사흘째나 기척이 없던 것이었다.

나는 눈부신 햇살이 유리창의 성에를 잘폭하게 녹여갈 때쯤 해서야 부스스 일어나 앉았다. 햇살보다 더 눈이 시린 가녀린 손가락이 조형해낼 뜻 모를 그림들을 기대해보던 나는 점점 멋쩍어갔다.

나는 방을 나와 개울을 향해 걸었다. 눈밭은 소록대는 함박눈을 쌓아 재울 뿐 어느 한곳에도 그 눈꽃들은 피어 있지 않았다.

나는 그 눈꽃들이 결을 이루던 길목을 짐작하며 오랜

flakes. Although I had been watching the window for three dawns, the woman's strange pictures stopped appearing.

I dragged myself up when the sun began melting away the frost into tiny pieces from my window. I felt more and more awkward for expecting those incomprehensible pictures to appear, for hoping to see that pale thin finger that blinded my eyes even more than the morning's brilliant sunrays.

I came out of my shack and walked towards the brook. The snow was piling up in the snowfield. There were now no snow-flowers blooming any-where.

I walked, leaving large footprints on the path where the snow-flowers used to bloom. It was like the careful outing of an innocent mountain animal.

The gray sky hung low and gloomy, sending a blanket of heavy snow flying. The snow piled over the large rocks that protruded over the brook, muffling the trickling sound of water under the torn ice layers. I watched the snow disappear between the ice layers through the cracks of the large rock and shook my body like a pheasant shaking off the morning dew. I was feeling relieved after I finished urinating into the snow.

만에 크고 넓은 내 발도장을 찍어대며 걷고 있었다. 천진한 산짐승의 조심스러운 나들이처럼—.

잿빛 하늘은 낮게 우중충대며 함박눈을 날리우고 있었고 찢긴 얼음결 속의 졸졸대는 개울물 소리를 감추고 앉은 왕돌더미 위로 그 함박눈들이 소복이 쌓여가고 있었다.

나는 왕돌 틈새의 얼음결 속으로 사그라드는 눈송이들에게 눈길을 던진 채 이슬을 털어내는 장끼처럼 부르르 몸을 떨었다.

막 후련한 소변을 보고난 참이었다.

나의 눈길이 눈발 속에 갇힌 개울 끝쯤의 혜자네 판잣집께를 내려다보며 허망하게 떠 있었을 때, 마침 혜자가 그 눈발 속을 실러 깡충깡충 뛰어오고 있었다.

혜자는 내 앞에 이르러 잠시 하늘 속을 올려다봤다. 그러고 나서 내 발치 밑의 눈밭 위에다 눈길을 떨궜다.

"어디 아팠니?"

"……."

"사흘 동안 꼼짝 않고 뭘 했니?"

혜자는 나의 말에 대꾸도 않고 여전히 내 발치 밑에다만 눈길을 모으고 있었다. 혜자는 뭔가 한참 골똘하

While I looked in the area of Hye-ja's shack, at Hye-ja's home hunched near the end of the brook, imprisoned under the pouring snow, I spied Hye-ja hopping towards me, moving through the whirling mass of descending snowflakes. When she got within a few feet of me Hye-ja looked up at the sky for a moment, then looked down around my feet.

"Were you sick? What have you been doing for the past three days?" I asked.

She didn't answer. Instead, Hye-ja continued staring at the area around my feet. After seeming to consider something for a while, she leaned over, and, to my surprise, began to make footprints with her tiny rubber shoes from out of the yellow imprint my urine had made. After that, she imprinted petals with roundish grains one by one, beginning with the spot next to the first footprint.

Her face was a little listless as she did this and so looked more pitiful than usual. Hye-ja carefully made petals, slowly whirling around like the second hand of an electric watch. Hye-ja finished the last of the snow-flower petals that bloomed at the tip of her foot, a flower that had yellow pistils in its center. I looked down at Hye-ja casually, and sud-

게 생각하는 눈치더니 이내 나의 오줌발이 뚫어놓은 노란색 구멍에서부터 앙증맞도록 작고 귀여운 고무신 자국을 내는 거였다. 그리고 나선 그 첫 번째 고무신 자국에서부터 차례로 결이 영근 꽃잎을 새겨가고 있었다.

혜자는 다소 맥이 빠진 듯한, 그래서 여느 때보다도 더 측은해 뵈는 그런 얼굴로 전자시계의 초침처럼 천천히 맴돌이를 하며 정성껏 꽃잎을 만들어가고 있는 것이었다.

혜자의 발끝에서 피어나고 있는 노란색 꽃술의 눈꽃이 마지막 꽃잎을 채웠을 때였다. 나는 혜자의 그런 모습을 예사스럽게 보아 넘기다 말고 문득 모가지께에다 차디찬 소름을 얹었다.

"……무슨 꽃이지?"

"몰라요!"

나는 혜자의 작은 고무신이 찍어대는, 그 애의 작은 고무신 코에서부터 펴나고 있는 이름 모를 꽃잎들을 보면서부터 한 가지 섬뜩한 기억을 떠올리고 있던 것이었다. 그 기억이 미처 여물기도 전에 혜자가 낮게 말했던 것이다.

"할머니가 그러는데요…… 우리 엄마요. 지금 막 죽

denly I felt goosebumps across my neck.

"What kind of flowers are these?" I asked.

"I don't know."

I suddenly remembered something chilling as I watched Hye-ja scurry around and as that nameless flower bloomed from the tip of her tiny rubber shoes. Even before this memory could fully take shape, though, Hye-ja said in a low voice, "Grandma said... my mom, you know, she just died!"

I said nothing.

Then, I reached down and hugged Hye-ja abruptly. I stared blankly in the direction of Hye-ja's shack through the shroud of descending snow.

Hye-ja lifted her face and stared up at me. After a while, she wriggled out of my arms and began articulating clearly, "I'm going to be so bored now... Please pee for me instead of my mom. I'll make flowers... My mom, you know, she got tired of walking so fast that she peed every few steps... So, Grandma told me to follow Mom whenever Mom went to your house and to draw snow-flowers after Mom peed so that it wouldn't show... Now, please pee for me, please, Uncle!"

I couldn't answer.

"I mean it. I'll make snow-flowers... You think I'm

었대요!"

"⋯⋯?"

나는 혜자의 어깻죽지를 와락 싸안았다. 그리고 눈발
속으로 먼 혜자네 집을 허망하게 바라다볼 뿐이었다.

혜자가 얼굴을 들어 나를 빤히 올려다봤다. 한동안 그
러고 있던 혜자가 나의 팔아름을 빠져나가며 시무룩해
진 얼굴로 또록또록 말을 이었다.

"나 인제 심심하겠다아⋯⋯ 엄마 대신 인제 아저씨가
오줌 싸줘요. 내가 꽃 만들어줄게요. ⋯⋯우리 엄마는
요, 쪼금만 걸어두요, 힘이 없어서 오줌을 막 싼대요.
⋯⋯그래서 할머니가요, 날 보고요 엄마가 아저씨 집
에 갈 때는 꼭 따라다니면서요, 엄마가 오줌 누고 나면
표 안 나게요, 눈꽃을 만들랬어요. ⋯⋯인제 아저씨가
오줌 싸줘요, 네에?"

"⋯⋯."

"진짜예요. 내가 눈꽃 만들어줄 거예요. ⋯⋯거짓말
인 줄 아나봐, 피―."

혜자는 몇 번 내 얼굴을 흘끔거리더니 이내 바지 주
머니에다 두 손을 찔렀다. 그러고 나서 놀이터에 놀러
가는 아이처럼 흔연스럽게 깡충대며 집을 향해 갔다.

lying? No way!"

After glancing at me sideways a few times, Hye-ja put her hands into her pant pockets. Then, she leapt lightly back towards her shack like a child making her way to a playground.

I looked around after she left and all I saw was my long train of parallel footprints. They stretched from the shack with my little room in it to the brook, and the snow flew in great powdery billows together with the fluttering crossbills, and the gentle trembling of the ripe pine needles that sent the crossbills off on their winter flight.

Translated by Jeon Seung-hee

내 눈 안으로 드는 것들은, 내 사글셋방 쪽에서부터 개울까지 나란히 패인 내 긴 발자국들과 잣새들의 푸득거림에 흩날리는 눈가루, 그리고 그 잣새들을 날려보내고 난 영근 솔잎들의 하들하들 떨어대는 연한 미동들뿐이었다.

『저녁의 게임 외』, 한국소설의 얼굴 10, 푸른사상, 2013

해설

Afterword

고통의 미학

황정산 (문학평론가)

천승세는 1960, 70년대 한국의 민중문학을 대표하는
작가이다. 천승세의 작품들은 대부분 우리 사회의 최하
층 민중들이 겪고 있는 삶의 피폐한 현실을 보여준다.
특히 6, 70년대는 한국사회가 급격한 산업화를 경험한
시대이다. 이 시기를 거쳐 경제발전을 이룬 것은 사실
이지만 또 한편에서는 많은 민중들이 원래 살던 농촌사
회의 몰락과 함께 도시로 몰려들어 빈민층을 형성하게
된다. 천승세의 소설은 바로 이 하층 빈민계급들의 삶
의 애환을 비장하게 그려냈다. 「혜자의 눈꽃」은 이런 그
의 작품 세계와 맥을 같이 하고 있으면서도 한층 미학
적인 완성도를 보여주는 작품이다.

Aesthetics of Pain

Hwang Jeong-san (literary critic)

Chun Seung-sei is a writer representative of the 1960s and the 1970s Korean *minjung* era in literature. Most of his works depict the bitter lives of those on the lowest rungs of Korean society. The 1960s and the 1970s were a period of rapid industrialization in Korea. Although it was a period of economic development, it was also the period during which most people who once lived in the countryside began to crowd the urban areas and began to settle in as the new urban lower class. Chun Seung-sei's works depict the joys and sorrows in the tragic lives of people from this class. "Hye-ja's Snow-Flowers" is one of Chun Seung-sei's

소설 속 주인공 '나'는 도시 변두리 판자촌에 기거하면서 혜자네 식구들을 만나게 된다. 혜자 엄마는 정신병과 폐병을 함께 앓고 있는 중증 환자이다. 환자라기보다는 죽어가고 있는 사람에 가깝다고 할 수 있다. 어느날 그녀는 '나'의 집에 찾아와 성에 낀 유리창을 화판으로 삼아 알 수 없는 무늬를 그린다. 그리고 그러한 행위는 그 후 계속 반복된다. 그런데 그럴 때마다 뒤따라오는 혜자가 그녀의 발자국에 자신의 발자국을 더해 꽃을 만들어놓는다. 더 이상한 일은 그렇게 만들어진 눈꽃 가운데에 꼭 노란 꽃술이 그려져 있다는 것이다.

'나'는 혜자 엄마가 죽고 난 후에야 혜자의 입을 통해 그 사연의 전말을 알게 된다. 병이 심해져 점점 죽어가는 혜자 엄마의 몸에서 설금찔금 새는 오줌의 흔적을 지우기 위해 혜자 할머니가 혜자로 하여금 그렇게 하도록 시킨 것이다. 혜자 할머니는 그 오줌 흔적이 추한 것으로 보이지 않게 하기 위해 자기 손녀로 하여금 아름다운 눈꽃을 만들도록 한 것이다. 이 눈꽃은 바로 죽어가는 혜자 엄마의 고통을 말해주는 것이기도 하지만 그 죽음의 고통을 아름답게 승화시킨 꽃이기도 하다.

혜자 엄마와 그 가족은 6, 70년대 한국사회의 빈민층

masterpieces in this category.

The main character and narrator of this story encounters Hye-ja's family while living in a shantytown on the outskirts of Seoul. Hye-ja's mother suffers from both tuberculosis and psychosis, but, unlike other ordinary patients of these afflictions, Hye-ja's mother is about to die. She shows up outside the narrator's room window one day and draws unrecognizable pictures on its frosted surface. This kind of visit repeats for some time. Interestingly, after every visit, she also leaves imprints of tiny snowflowers behind, snowflowers Hye-ja must have imprinted on the snowfield with her tiny feet. Also strangely, there are always yellow pistils in the middle of each of these flowers.

The narrator learns how Hye-ja must have imprinted those flowers after Hye-ja's mother died. Through Hye-ja's innocent intimations, he discovers that Hye-ja's grandmother let Hye-ja imprint petals with her feet in order to hide her ailing mother's urine stains on the snow. Hye-ja's grandmother wanted to turn the traces of her incontinence from something dirty and ugly to something beautiful. These snowflowers represent not only the pain the dying woman must have experienced

을 대변한다고 할 수 있다. 이들은 과거 자신들의 삶의 터전인 농촌이나 어촌에서 떠나와 도시 변두리에 판잣집을 짓고 힘든 하루하루의 삶을 살아가는 최하층 민중들이라 할 수 있다. 혜자 엄마가 앓고 있는 정신병과 폐병은 이들 민중들의 정신과 육체의 상태를 상징적으로 말해주는 것이기도 하다. 가혹한 삶의 조건과 궁핍한 경제 사정은 그들의 몸과 생활을 병들게 했을 것이고, 전통적인 공동체를 빼앗긴 이들의 삶은 또한 어떤 정신적 지향도 가지기 힘들었을 것이다. 이들이 건강한 육체와 건전한 정신을 가지지 못한 것은 바로 산업화라는 명목으로 이들을 변두리의 가혹한 삶의 환경으로 내몬 당시 사회적 요구 때문이다.

하지만 작가는 죽음으로 끝나는 이들의 고통을 어둠과 좌절로만 묘사하지 않는다. 여기에 이 소설의 묘미가 놓여 있다. 점점 죽음으로 다가가는 병을 앓으며 그 병 때문에 보일 수밖에 없는 혜자 엄마의 추한 모습을 그들의 가족은 아름다움으로 지우고자 했다. 그것은 바로 착취와 그에 따른 가난 속에서도 결코 아름다움을 포기하지 않으려는 민중들의 삶의 자세를 보여준다. 그것을 통해 민중들은 자신들의 존재와 정체성을 포기하

but also its sublimation into something beautiful.

Hye-ja's mother and her family were typical of the Korean urban poor class in the 1960s and 1970s. As members of the lowest class, they led trying lives in the shantytowns on the outskirts of cities after being driven out of the countryside or seashore areas. The psychosis and tuberculosis that Hye-ja's mother suffers from symbolize the mental and physical hardships those people endured. Their harsh living conditions and dire financial situations were sure to lead to deteriorated health conditions, and the loss of traditional communities likely led to a spiritual or mental void. The society that drives them to harsh living environment under the banner of industrialization made it impossible for them to stay healthy both physically and mentally.

Still, the author does not depict their painful lives that end in death as something only depressing and frustrating. Herein lies the beauty of this story. Hye-ja's family tries successfully to erase the ugly byproducts of Hye-ja's mother's terminal illness by turning it into something beautiful. This is symbolic of these people's attitude towards life, one that prevents them from ever forgetting beauty in the

지 않고 자신들의 삶이 보여줄 수 있는 또 다른 아름다움을 만들어낸다. 작가 천승세는 바로 여기에서 새로운 가능성을 발견하고 있다. 고통이 아름다움으로 승화될 때 변두리 빈민인 민중들의 삶 역시 역사적 의미를 가지게 된다는 점을 작가는 우리에게 말해주고 있다. 이 작품은 전체적으로 서정적이고 또한 미학적이다. 하지만 그 서정과 미학을 작가는 당대 현실의 모습에서 찾는다. 그럼으로써 당대 현실의 모순과 문제점을 극복해 나갈 새로운 미학과 윤리를 우리에게 던져준다.

midst of their poverty-stricken, exploited, ugly lives. They refuse to give up on themselves and lose their identities, creating something beautiful out of whatever lives they lead. Chun Seung-sei finds a positive outlook from the harsh reality of their times. He also tells us that the lives of the marginalized urban poor acquire historical meaning in the moment of sublimating pain into beauty. Overall, "Hye-ja's Snow-Flowers" is a lyrical and aesthetically triumphant story. It is remarkable that the author could create this kind of story out of the harsh reality of his times. This leads us to a new aesthetics and system of ethics that will guide us to imagine a future beyond the contradictions and problems of our reality.

비평의 목소리

Critical Acclaim

천승세는 도시 변두리의 가난한 서민, 농민, 양공주, 무당 등 다양한 소재들을 다루지만 특히 어민들의 생활을 그리는 데에 독보적인 역량을 발휘하는 듯하다. 작품집 『황구의 비명』에서도 이 계열의 중편 「낙월도」와 희곡 「만선」에 특별한 무게가 주어져 있고, 그의 소설집 『신궁』에서도 「백중날」이나 「종돈」 같은 농촌소설과 더불어 책의 표제로 되어 있는 중편 「신궁」이 뛰어난 성과를 내고 있다.

그의 작품들에서 우리가 받는 첫인상은 그 뻑뻑한 토속성이다. 그것은 단순히 사투리가 많이 쓰이고 있다는 것만을 의미하지 않는다. 물론 그의 작품들에는 일반

Chun Seung-sei has dealt with the lives of the urban poor, farmers, prostitutes catering to Westerners, and shamans. Among all these various people's lives, his touch is the most uniquely outstanding when depicting fishermen's lives. His novella, *The Nakwol Island,* and play, "A Large Catch" from Chun's fiction collection, *Cry of a Yellow Dog*, as well as, his novella, *Divine Arrow,* from his fiction collection, *Divine Arrow,* are all fine stories that deal with fishermen's lives.

The most immediately apparent characteristic of his works is their heavily folkloric quality. This quality does not come simply from his frequent use

독자들에게 익숙지 않은 사투리와 무속적인 용어들이 대량으로 등장하고 있어, 때로는 그 때문에 얼른 이해되지 않는 대목조차 있다. 그러나 이런 고충을 견디고 읽어나가노라면 우리는 그 토속적 어휘들 속에 형상화된 강력한 토속적 인간상을 만나게 된다. 이 경우 천승세 문학의 뛰어난 점은 토속성이 결코 어떤 복고주의나 전원 취미를 지향하지 않는다는 사실, 다시 말해서 그 토속성이 근대문명과 국가조직의 혜택에서 소외된 민중적 삶의 실감을 포착하려는 문학적 촉수로서 기능한다는 사실이다.

염무웅

천승세 소설의 일관성은 비극적 민중현실을 다루는 데 있다. 그런데 같은 민중현실이라 할지라도, 「신궁」에 나타난 어민들의 거친 현실과 「혜자의 눈꽃」에 담긴 도시 변두리 인생들의 애잔한 모습은 별 연관성이 없어 보인다. 그러나 전통적 토속세계에 대한 깊은 애정과 연민이 천승세 소설의 본령임을 알아챘다면, 이 두 작품 간의 연관 역시 자연스럽게 이해할 수 있다. (중략) 당시 급속하게 진행되던 근대화 과정에 대해 작가가 대

of regional dialects. To be sure, his stories feature frequent use of dialects and shamanistic terms ordinary readers might not be familiar with and, occasionally, may not even readily understand. If we get past these obstacles, though, we meet powerful folkloric human beings embedded in these dialects and shamanistic terms. What makes Chun's literature stand out is that this folkloric quality does not take us to a reactionary and pastoral direction. Instead, it functions as literary feelers that capture the solid reality of marginalized people who are excluded from the benefits of modern civilization and state structure.

Yeom Mu-ung

The novelist Chun Seung-sei is consistently interested in the tragic reality of ordinary people's lives. At first glance, the fishermen's difficult reality in *Divine Arrow* and the fragile lives of the urban poor in "Hye-ja's Snow-Flowers," do not seem to have anything in common, although they are both ordinary people's lives. However, if we remember that Chun Seung-sei's main concern comes from his deep affection and sympathy for the traditional folkloric world, we can easily see the connection

단히 비판적인 시각을 가진 것은 당연하다. 사람살이의 기본을 망가뜨리는 일이었으니까. 그 망가진 삶의 모습이 도시 변두리의 소시민한테서 보일 때,「혜자의 눈꽃」에서와 같은 애잔한 비극성을 띠게 된다. 아마도 장선포 같은 어느 어촌 또는 농촌을 떠나 도시로 흘러들어왔을 혜자네 가족의 비극적이고도 쓸쓸한 삶의 모습이야말로, 공동체 파괴가 무엇을 의미하는지를 잘 보여준다.

정홍섭

산업화가 본격적으로 진행된 1970년대의 시점에서 볼 때 천승세가 관심을 갖는 토속적인 세계나 도시 변두리는 근대의 담론을 주도하는 중심적 공간과는 구별되는 공간이다. 근대적인 도시에서 멀리 떨어진 농어촌이나 혹은 도시와 인접해 있되 철저히 배제되는 변두리는 근대화의 수혜를 제대로 입지 못하면서도 산업사회의 모순이 중층적으로 얽혀 있는 복합적인 공간이기도 하다. 이러한 지역적 불평등은 근대화에 가속도가 붙을수록 오히려 심화되어 왔다. 천승세는 소외된 민중의 현실과 그들이 속한 사회의 은폐된 모순을 작품 속에 부조한다.

between the two stories...

It seems natural that Chun Seung-sei was critical of the rapid modernization of those times, this revolution so often destroying the very basic values and qualities of so many people's lives. Those destroyed lives embodied in the lives of the urban petit bourgeoisie took the form of the delicate tragedy shown in "Hye-ja's Snow-Flowers." The tragic, desolate life Hye-ja's family leads in the outskirts of the city—perhaps, after being driven out of a fishing village like Jangseonpo from *Divine Arrow*—superbly illustrates what it means to destroy a community.

Jeong Hong-seop

From the perspective of the Korean industrialization period of the 1970's, Chun Seung-sei's folkloric world or outer city areas seem like a world altogether different from the dominant space that has traditionally led the discourse of modernity. Farming or fishing villages far away from modern cities, the outskirts of cities, spaces close to, yet thoroughly disconnected from them, are complex spaces that rarely benefit from modernization. Rather, these are spaces where the various contra-

이 때문에 그의 소설은 1970년대 산업화에 대한 비판적 성찰을 동반한 작품이 대부분이다. 주의할 점은 소위 근대성에 대한 비판이 전근대적 삶의 방식에 대한 무조건적인 옹호로 기울거나 과거를 그리워하는 낭만적인 향수로 직결된 것이 아니라는 사실이다. 작가가 그리는 농어촌의 모습은 도시인의 시각에서 그리는 아름답고 풍요로운 이상과는 거리가 멀기 때문이다. 작가가 포착한 민중적 공간은 이미 가난과 원한, 불신과 살의가 미만한 처절한 생존의 전장에 가깝다.

양윤의

dictions of industrialized society are intertwined. This kind of regional inequality has intensified as the speed of modernization has accelerated. Chun Seung-sei has superbly carved into his works the reality of ordinary people alienated from the modernization process, exposing the hidden contradictions in larger society itself. Thus, most of Chun Seung-sei's works include his critical reflections on 1970s industrialization. It is noteworthy that his reflections on modernity do not mean that he approves the pre-modern way of life unconditionally or indulges in nostalgia. The farming or fishing villages the author depicts are far from the beautiful and affluent utopias idealized by urban dwellers. In fact, those spaces, captured by the author, are closer to battlefields where people fight for their survival amidst poverty, grudges, distrust, and murderous ill-will.

Yang Yun-ui

천승세

천승세(千勝世)는 1939년 2월 23일 여류 소설가 박화성의 둘째 아들로 전라남도 목포에서 태어났다. 목포에서 목포고등학교를 졸업하고 가족과 함께 서울로 올라온 뒤 1958년 《동아일보》 신춘문예에 소설 「점례와 소」가, 1964년 《경향신문》 신춘문예에 희곡 「물꼬」가 그리고 같은 해 국립극장 현상문예에 희곡 「만선」이 각각 당선되었다. 1990년에는 계간지 《창작과비평》에 십여 편의 시를 발표하면서 시인으로도 등단했다. 1961년 성균관대학교 국문학과를 졸업하고 《신태양사》 기자, 문화방송 전속작가, 《한국일보》 기자를 지냈으며, 1980년대 초에는 민족문학작가회의(현 한국작가회의)의 자유실천위원장을 지내기도 하면서 진보적 문화운동에도 활발하게 참여하여 왔다.

그는 토착적인 세계와 그 안의 민중들의 삶을 사실적인 묘사로 보여줌으로써 근대화와 산업화 과정에서 소외된 주변 민중들의 고통을 대변하는 작품을 써왔다. 토속적인 언어로 어촌의 서정적인 모습과 어민들의 궁

Chun Seung-sei

Chun Seung-sei was born in 1939 in Mokpo, Je-ollanam-do as the second son of the renowned novelist Park Hwa-seong. After graduating from Mokpo High School, he moved to Seoul with his family. He made his literary debut in 1958, when his short story "Jeomnye and a Cow" won the 1958 *Dong-A Ilbo* Spring Literary Contest. He also made his stage debut in 1964, when his play "An Irrigation Gate" won the 1964 *Kyunghyang Shinmun* Spring Literary Contest. He also won the National Theatre of Korea Prize with his play "A Large Catch" the same year. In addition, he made his poetry debut in 1990, when about ten of his poems were published in the literary *Quarterly Changbi*. After graduating from the Department of Korean Language and Literature, SungKyunKwan University, he worked as a reporter for the *Sintaeyang* magazine company, as a staff writer for the Munhwa Broadcasting Company, and as a reporter for the *Hankook Ilbo*. He has participated actively in progressive cultural movement, working, for example, as the chair of the Freedom

핍한 삶을 실감나게 묘사한「신궁」과 가난한 농촌에서 상경하여 서울 변두리 기지촌에서 미군을 상대로 몸을 팔아야 하는 한 여인의 삶을 그린「황구의 비명」, 도시 변두리로 흘러든 가난한 주변부 인생의 죽음을 아름답게 형상화한「혜자의 눈꽃」등이 대표작이다. 단편소설집으로는『감루연습』(1978),『황구의 비명』(1975),『신궁』(1977),『혜자의 눈꽃』(1978) 등과 중편소설집『낙월도』(1972), 장편소설집『낙과를 줍는 기린』(1978),『해척원보전』,『사계의 후조 (상,하)』(1977),『깡돌이의 서울』(1973) 등이 있다. 그밖에 콩트집으로『대중탕의 피카소』(1983), 수필집으로『꽃병 물 좀 갈까요』(1979) 등이 있다. 1965년「만선」으로 제1회 한국연극영화예술상(백상예술상 개칭)을 수상했으며,『혜사의 눈꽃』으로 이상문학상(1978)과 비평가상을 수상했으며, 자유문학상 본상(1989), 성옥문학상 대상(1982)을 수상했다. 1975년「황구의 비명」과「폭염」으로 만해문학상(1982)을 수상하였다. 2000년도부터는 고향인 목포로 내려가 작품 활동을 계속하며 살고 있다.

Practice Committee at the Association of Writers for National Literature during the early 1980s.

Chun Seung-sei has been producing works that realistically represent the difficult lives of the marginalized people ordinarily excluded from the process of modernization and industrialization. He is most well-known for *Divine Arrow*, a vivid lyrical depiction of a folkloric fishing village and the fishermen's poverty-stricken lives, "Cry of a Yellow Dog," a story of a woman who ends up selling her body to U.S. soldiers after her poverty-driven expulsion from the countryside, and "Hye-ja's Snow-Flowers," a beautiful depiction of the death of a woman and her poor, marginalized family on the outskirt of Seoul. His published works include short story collections, *Practicing Tears of Gratitude* (1978), *Cry of a Yellow Dog* (1975), *Divine Arrow* (1977), and *Hye-ja's Snow-Flowers* (1978); the novella collection *The Nakwol Island* (1972); and the novels *Giraffe Picking Up Fallen Fruits* (1978), *Migrants of Four Seasons* (1977), and *Kkangdori's Seoul* (1973). Additionally, he wrote a short-short story collection *Picasso at the Public Bath* (1983) and an essay collection *Shall We Change Water in the Vase?* (1970). He won the first Korean Drama and Film Art Award (later, Baeksang Arts Award) for his play "A Large Catch" in 1965, the Yi Sang Literary Award and the Critics' Award for "Hye-ja's Snow-Flowers" in 1978, and the Manhae Literary Award for "Cry of a Yellow Dog" and "Summer Heat" in 1975. His other awards include the Freedom Literary Award(1989), the Seong-ok Literary Award(1982). He has been living and writing in Mokpo, his hometown, since 2000.

번역 **전승희** Translated by Jeon Seung-hee

전승희는 서울대학교와 하버드대학교에서 영문학과 비교문학으로 박사 학위를 받았으며, 현재 하버드대학교 한국학 연구소의 연구원으로 재직하며 아시아 문예 계간지 《ASIA》 편집위원으로 활동 중이다. 현대 한국문학 및 세계문학을 다룬 논문을 다수 발표했으며, 바흐친의 『장편소설과 민중언어』, 제인 오스틴의 『오만과 편견』 등을 공역했다. 1988년 한국여성연구소의 창립과 《여성과 사회》의 창간에 참여했고, 2002년부터 보스턴 지역 피학대 여성을 위한 단체인 '트랜지션하우스' 운영에 참여해 왔다. 2006년 하버드대학교 한국학 연구소에서 '한국 현대사와 기억'을 주제로 한 워크숍을 주관했다.

Jeon Seung-hee is a member of the Editorial Board of *ASIA*, and a Fellow at the Korea Institute, Harvard University. She received a Ph.D. in English Literature from Seoul National University and a Ph.D. in Comparative Literature from Harvard University. She has presented and published numerous papers on modern Korean and world literature. She is also a co-translator of Mikhail Bakhtin's *Novel and the People's Culture* and Jane Austen's *Pride and Prejudice*. She is a founding member of the Korean Women's Studies Institute and of the biannual Women's Studies' journal *Women and Society* (1988), and she has been working at 'Transition House,' the first and oldest shelter for battered women in New England. She organized a workshop entitled "The Politics of Memory in Modern Korea" at the Korea Institute, Harvard University, in 2006. She also served as an advising committee member for the Asia-Africa Literature Festival in 2007 and for the POSCO Asian Literature Forum in 2008.

감수 **데이비드 윌리엄 홍** Edited by David William Hong

데이비드 윌리엄 홍은 미국 일리노이주 시카고에서 태어났다. 일리노이대학교에서 영문학을, 뉴욕대학교에서 영어교육을 공부했다. 지난 2년간 서울에 거주하면서 처음으로 한국인과 아시아계 미국인 문학에 깊이 몰두할 기회를 가졌다. 현재 뉴욕에서 거주하며 강의와 저술 활동을 한다.

David William Hong was born in 1986 in Chicago, Illinois. He studied English Literature at the University of Illinois and English Education at New York University. For the past two years, he lived in Seoul, South Korea, where he was able to immerse himself in Korean and Asian-American literature for the first time. Currently, he lives in New York City, teaching and writing.

바이링궐 에디션 한국 대표 소설 051
혜자의 눈꽃

2014년 3월 7일 초판 1쇄 인쇄 | 2014년 3월 14일 초판 1쇄 발행

지은이 천승세 | 옮긴이 전승희 | 펴낸이 김재범
감수 데이비드 윌리엄 홍 | 기획 정은경, 전성태, 이경재
편집 정수인, 이은혜 | 관리 박신영 | 디자인 이춘희
펴낸곳 (주)아시아 | 출판등록 2006년 1월 27일 제406-2006-000004호
주소 서울특별시 동작구 서달로 161-1(흑석동 100-16)
전화 02.821.5055 | 팩스 02.821.5057 | 홈페이지 www.bookasia.org
ISBN 979-11-5662-002-0 (set) | 979-11-5662-008-2 (04810)
값은 뒤표지에 있습니다.

Bi-lingual Edition Modern Korean Literature 051
Hye-ja's Snow-Flowers

Written by Chun Seung-sei | Translated by Jeon Seung-hee
Published by Asia Publishers | 161-1, Seodal-ro, Dongjak-gu, Seoul, Korea
Homepage Address www.bookasia.org | Tel. (822).821.5055 | Fax. (822).821.5057
First published in Korea by Asia Publishers 2014
ISBN 979-11-5662-002-0 (set) | 979-11-5662-008-2 (04810)